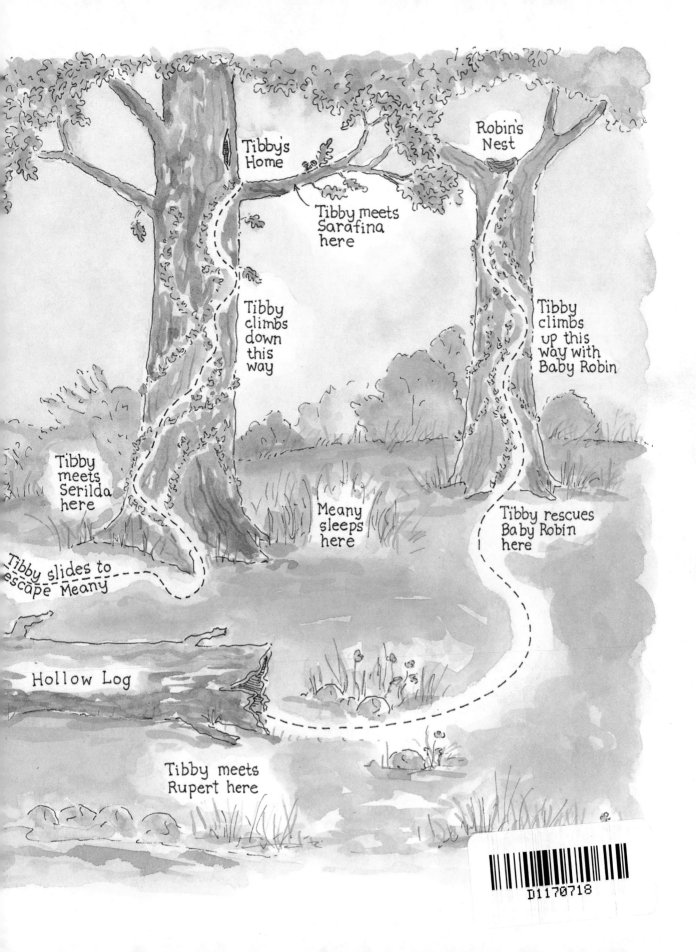

Tibby Tried It

To our beloved teachers Alex,
Emily, Will, and Taylor ... and
all the blessed children from
whom we learn— S.U. and E.U.

For Jim and Seth—C.P.

Published by
MAGINATION PRESS
An Educational Publishing Foundation Book
American Psychological Association
750 First Street, NE
Washington, DC 20002

For more information about our books, including a complete catalog, please write to us, call 1-800-374-2721, or visit our website at www.maginationpress.com.

Editor: Darcie Conner Johnston
Art Director: Susan K. White
The text type is New Century Schoolbook
Printed by R.R. Donnelley & Sons, Willard, Ohio

Library of Congress Cataloging-in-Publication Data

Useman, Sharon.
Tibby tried it / Sharon and Ernie Useman ; illustrated by Cary Pillo.
        p.   cm.
Summary: Tibby the tree swallow cannot fly because he has a crooked wing, but the other animals teach him skills that come in handy when a baby robin falls from its nest.
ISBN 1-55798-558-8 (cloth)
[1. Tree swallow—Fiction. 2. Swallows—Fiction. 3. Animals—Fiction.]
I. Useman, Ernie. II. Pillo, Cary, ill. III. Title.
PZ7.U695Ti 1998
                                          [E]—dc21 98-39702
                                                    CIP
                                                    AC

First Edition
Manufactured in the United States of America
10 9 8 7 6 5 4 3 2 1

Tibby Tried It

written by
Sharon and Ernie Useman

illustrated by
Cary Pillo

MAGINATION PRESS • WASHINGTON, DC

This is Tibby Tree Swallow.
Most tree swallows fly very high
and fast, soaring and dipping and
catching insects in the air for their
food. But Tibby can't fly, because
he was born with a crooked wing.

Sometimes Tibby felt lonely because the other birds didn't talk to him, so he stayed close to home in the hollow of an old oak tree. One day when Mama Tree Swallow saw the sad look on Tibby's face, she quietly called to him, "Please come in, Tibby, I have something to give you."

Tibby's mother opened her treasure chest and took out a cloth. "Tibby, use this special cloth wisely, and you can learn to do many wonderful things."

"But, Mama, how will this cloth help me?" he asked.

"I'm sure you will find a way," Mama lovingly said.

Tibby took Mama's gift outside.
"Maybe the other birds will
talk to me if they can't see my
crooked wing," he thought.
So he covered it with the cloth.

As Tibby sat watching the other birds fly, a red squirrel jumped on the branch with him. "Hello," she said cheerfully, "I'm Sarafina Squirrel and I can climb trees."

Tibby was so happy to make a new friend that he forgot all about hiding his wing. "Pleased to meet you!" he chirped, "I'm Tibby Tree Swallow."

"It's nice to meet you, too, Tibby," said Sarafina.
"Would you like to come down to the ground with me?
There are lots of exciting things for you to see."

"I have a crooked wing and I can't fly," Tibby told her.
"How can I get down to the ground?"

"Come, I'll show you how to climb," she said.

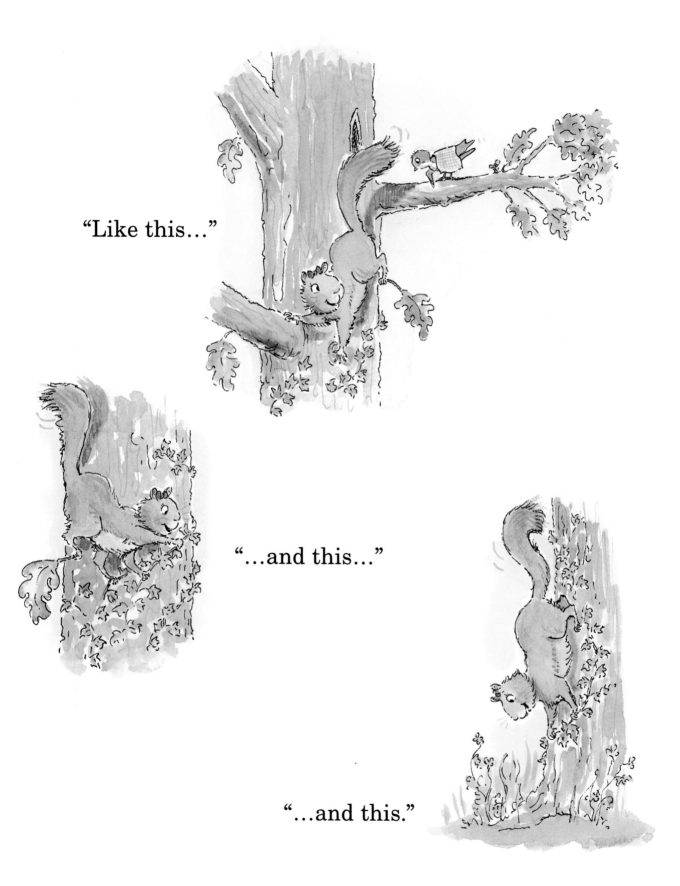

"Like this…"

"…and this…"

"…and this."

So Tibby tried it.

First, he tied the cloth around his neck.

"Are you afraid?" asked Sarafina.

"Just a little," said Tibby.

"That's okay, you're doing fine," said Sarafina.

"I can't fly," Tibby thought to himself, "but I can climb!"

The other tree swallows
settled on nearby branches
to watch. Surprised at the
sight of Tibby climbing down
a tree, they began to laugh.

Tibby heard the birds laughing,
but he said to himself, "I am going
to keep on climbing."

Suddenly, Sarafina shouted, "Watch
out, Tibby, don't step on Serilda!"

"Oh! Who are you?" asked Tibby.

"I'm S-s-serilda S-s-snake, and I s-s-slide," she smiled.

"How do you do that?" he asked.

"Come, I'll s-s-show you," said Serilda with a wink. "These are s-s-special s-s-slides I did when I was a circus s-s-star."

"How's this-s-s?"

"...and this-s-s?"

"...and this-s-s?"

So Tibby tried it.

"Now I can climb AND slide, Serilda!"

"Why, Tibby, you can s-s-slide better than my s-s-sister S-s-sonia!" she said.

And the other birds watched and laughed.

"Look up, Tibby, it's-s-s Rupert!"

"Hello! Who are you?" asked Tibby.

"I'm Rupert Rabbit, and I hop!" Rupert boasted.

"How do you do that?" Tibby wondered.

"Stand back, my boy, and let me show you some 'hip' hopping."

"Like this..."

"...and this..."

"...and this."

So Tibby tried it.

"Now I can climb and slide AND hop, Rupert!"

"Well, you're one whopper of a hopper, Tibby!"

And the other birds watched and laughed.

"Watch out, my boy,
don't hop on Hurricane!"

"Whoops! Who are you?" asked Tibby.

"I'm Hurricane Turtle," he whispered, "and I hide."

"How do you do that?" Tibby whispered back.

"Ssh-h, I'll show you," answered Hurricane.

"LIKE THIS…"

"…AND THIS…"

"…AND THIS."

26

So Tibby tried it.

"Hurricane, now I can climb and slide and hop AND hide!" he beamed.

"Your cloth makes a swell shell, Tibby," Hurricane said softly.

And the other birds watched and laughed.

"DO YOU HAVE ANY FLIES IN THERE?"

"Hey!" laughed Tibby. "Who are you?"

"Mi-mi-mi, I'm Caruso Frog and I zap flies," sang Caruso in a deep, loud voice.

"How do you do that?"

"Why, it's as easy as do-re-mi. I shall show you how."

EASY... EASY...

ZAP! "Ta-da!"

So Tibby tried it.

"Wow, Caruso, now I can climb and slide and hop and hide AND zap a fly!"

"Tibby, you are one zippidy-do-da zapper," crooned Caruso.

All of Tibby's new friends cheered.
But the other birds watched and laughed.

From her perch, Sarafina spied danger.

"Look out! It's Meany the Cat!" she cried.

"Hurry, Tibby,
climb the tree!"

"Mama, I had such fun today on the ground!"
Tibby panted, catching his breath. "I made lots of
new friends, and we all escaped Meany the Cat!"

"Meany the Cat!" Her eyes opened wide.
"Are you all right, Tibby?"

"Yes, Mama," he replied. "I got away all by myself."

Later, when Mama tucked Tibby in bed, she asked, "What did you do today with your new friends?"

Tibby's eyes sparkled. "I learned to climb and slide and hop and hide and zap a fly," he said. "But, Mama, the other birds laughed at me. Why did they laugh?"

Mama thought for a moment, then replied tenderly, "Well, Tibby, they believe birds should just fly."

"But, Mama, some birds can't fly," said Tibby as his eyes gently closed. "We *can* do other things, though."

The next morning, Tibby hurried
outside early, hoping to see some
of his new friends. "What a great
day this is going to be," he said
out loud, when suddenly he heard
Mrs. Robin in the next tree.
"Help! Help!" she cried.
"My baby fell out of the nest
and she can't fly!"

The other birds did
not know how to help.
But Tibby did. Quickly
he climbed down the
tree like Sarafina.

Tibby saw Meany sleeping
near the bottom of the tree.
Baby Robin was in great danger!

"I must get Meany away from
Baby Robin," thought Tibby,
and he slid like Serilda.

And he
hopped
like
Rupert.

And he
hid like
Hurricane.

"If Meany comes any closer
I can zap her on the nose!"
Tibby said fiercely to
himself as he headed toward
Baby Robin's tree.

At last Tibby reached Baby Robin
and wrapped her safely in his cloth.
"Don't be scared," he whispered.
"I'll get you home."

As fast as he could,
Tibby climbed up to
Mrs. Robin's nest. Now
the birds did not laugh.

That day everyone learned
that birds can do more than
just fly. All the birds sang
to celebrate … and Tibby
sang the loudest!

The End

ABOUT THE AUTHORS

Sharon and Ernie Useman live in Hammond, Louisiana. As a music therapist, Sharon's work with developmentally handicapped children inspired the theme for *Tibby Tried It*. The rest was provided through their grandchildren.

ABOUT THE ILLUSTRATOR

Cary Pillo grew up on a farm near the Cascade Mountains in Washington State. Surrounded by animals and birds, she began drawing them at an early age. Today she lives in Seattle with her husband and son, and like Tibby, she has a reputation for rescuing baby birds.